To Michael, David, and Chrissy—who love to wreak
havoc while Mom and Dad snore on
—K. W.

For Alan Baker, my tutor
—J. C.

SIMON &
SCHUSTER

First published in Great Britain in 2001 by Simon & Schuster UK Ltd
Africa House, 64 - 78 Kingsway, London WC2B 6AH

Text copyright © 2001 by Karma Wilson
Illustrations copyright © 2001 by Jane Chapman
Book design by Ann Bobco
The text of this book is set in Adobe Caslon.
The illustrations were rendered in acrylic paint.

A CIP catalogue record for this book is available from the British Library.

ISBN 0 689 83622 8

Printed in Hong Kong

1 3 5 7 9 10 8 6 4 2

Bear Snores On

Karma Wilson

illustrations by Jane Chapman

SIMON & SCHUSTER, LONDON

*I*n a cave in the woods, in his deep, dark lair, through the long, cold winter sleeps a great brown bear.

Cuddled in a heap, with his eyes shut tight,
he sleeps through the day, he sleeps through
the night.

The cold winds howl and the night sounds growl.

But
the bear
snores on.

An itty-bitty mouse, pitter-pat, tip-toe, creep-crawls
in the cave from the fluff-cold snow.

Mouse squeaks, "Too damp, too cold, too dark." So he lights wee twigs with a small, hot spark.

The twigs pip-pop and the wind doesn't stop.

But
the bear
snores on.

Two glowing eyes sneak-peek in the den.
Mouse cries, "Who's there?" and a hare hops in.

"Ho, Mouse!"
says Hare.
"Long time,
no see!"
So they pop
white corn.
And they brew
black tea.

Mouse sips wee slurps. Hare burps big BURPS!

But
the bear
snores on.

A badger scuttles by, sniff-snuffs at the air.
"I smell yummy-yums! Perhaps we can share?

"I've brought honey-nuts," Badger says with a grin.
"Let's divvy them up, settle down . . . and dig in!"

And they nibble and they munch with a

CHEW–

CHOMP–

CRUNCH!

But
the bear
snores on.

A vole and a mole tunnel up through the floor.
Then a wren and a raven flutter in through the door!

Mole mutters, "What a night!"
"What a storm!" twitters Wren.
And everybody clutters in the big bear's den.

They tweet and they titter. They chat and they chitter.

But
the bear
snores on.

*I*n a cave in the woods, a slumbering bear
sleeps through the party in his very own lair.

Hare stokes the fire. Mouse seasons stew.

Then a small pepper fleck makes the bear . . .

RAAAAA-CHOO

He blows and he sneezes,
and the whole crowd freezes . . .

And
the bear
WAKES UP!

BEAR GNARLS

and he SNARLS.

BEAR ROARS

and he RUMBLES!

BEAR JUMPS

and he STOMPS.

BEAR GROWLS

and he GRUMBLES!

"You've sneaked into my lair
and you've all had fun!
But me? I was sleeping
and . . .

I've had none!"

And he whimpers and he
moans, he wails and he groans . . .

And the bear blubbers on!

Mouse squeaks, "Don't fret. Don't fuss. Wait and see. We can pop more corn! We can brew more tea!"

Bear gulps. Bear gobbles. He sighs with delight. Then he spins tall tales through the blustery night.

When the sun peeks up on a crisp, clear dawn, Bear can't sleep . . .

But
his friends
snore on.